Rabbi Aron David Neustad
Rav Of Cong Klal Chasidim
Dayan Of Beis Din Givat Shaul
29 Zevion St Jerusalem
02-5849358   052-8982960

אהרן דוד נײשטאדט
רב דק"ק "קהל חסידים" נוה יעקב
חבר ב"ד ממרנות גבעת שאול
עיה"ק ירושלים ת"ו

בס"ד

My neighbor Rabbi Aryeh Mahr שליט"א presented these pages to me.

Its is a delightful work that displays Torah values in an interesting and informative style. A great kiruv and chinuch opportunity worthwhile to be printed.

with Blessings

אהרן ביג נײשטאדט

אהרן דוד נײשטאדט
רב דק"ק "קהל חסידים" נוה יעקב
רח' הרב זוין 29 טלפון: 02-5849358

כתובת רחוב זוין 29 נוה יעקב י-ם טל: 02-5849358 כתובת המשרד רחוב צפניה 39 י-ם פל: 0528-982960

My neighbor, Rabbi Aryeh Mahr presented these pages to me.
It is a delightful work that displays Torah Values in an interesting
and informative style.
A great Kiruv and Chinuch opportunity wirthwhile to be printed.

With Blessings
Aron Dovid Neustad

Rav of Cong Klal Chasidim
Dayan of Beis Din Givat Shaul

MAHRWOOD PRESS

Mahrwood Press

Stories and Reflections: Joe Kubert
Illustration: Joe Kubert
Graphics and Layout: Shmuel Kaffe
Lettering: Aryeh Mahr
Chief Editor: Akiva Atwood
Editor: Rabbi Reuven Schwartz
Commentary and Thoughts:
Miriam Samsonowitz,
Yehudis Schechtman
Inspiration: Rabbi Dr. Dovid Shalom Pape

Published by:

Mahrwood Press Ltd.
31 Zevin Street, Suite 8, Jerusalem, 97450
ISRAEL

Distributed in the US by:

FELDHEIM PUBLISHERS
208 Airport Executive Park
Nanuet, N.Y. 10954

Printed in Israel

1 2 3 4 5 6 7 8 9 10

Publisher's Forward

בס"ד

The book you are about to read and enjoy, is very special in many ways. The series of stories presented here have been wonderfully written and illustrated by Mr. Joe Kubert. When I first saw the stories and art that you will see unfold in these pages, what impressed me the most was how easily Joe was able to evoke the essence of each story. He can swing effortlessly from vivid depictions of Jewish history to the most mundane task of "koshering a pot". Each story in this book is an exciting adventure wrapped up in a few pages. But more than that each story has its own theme and teaches a valuable lesson about Yiddishkeit (Judaism) and life, made more powerful through his beautiful artwork and dynamic designs.

In cases where the boys, Yaakov and Isaac, are confronted with immediate decisions, or in instances where Halachah is discussed, in all cases, competent halachic (Jewish law) experts were consulted, both when Joe originally wrote and drew these stories, and during the preparation for this book. In real life situations it is important to consult with a competent Rabbi when making decisions or confronting problems such as those portrayed in our stories.

Joe envisioned a brief overview of how and why he produced each story. Early in the process, we decided that it would be a marvelous learning tool if we added an overview with questions and answers so that parents and teachers might enjoy these stories together with their children and students.

Some of my earliest memories of reading pleasure centered on specific dynamic stories and characters. To me, those particular stories and characters were more alive, more vital more exciting and entertaining. The figures were more fluid, the facial expressions more emotive like real people and not just figures on a page. The stories were more real, and the characters are all cultural icons. Joe Kubert is the artist and vision behind this book, as well as the innumerable stories I have spoken about. He is much more than a gentleman, he is a talented, kind hearted, learned and an upright man, with whom it is my pleasure and honor to have met and gotten to know. We are grateful that he allowed us to take on the project of producing this wonderful series of stories.

We are proud to present to you, "The Adventures of Yaakov and Isaac".

Aryeh Mahr
Mahrwood Press
Yerushalayim, Chanukah 5765

If you liked this book and would like to see more work from Mr. Joe Kubert, Send us your letters to:

Letters at Mahrwood Press
31 Zevin Street, Suite 8
Neve Yaakov, Jerusalem 97450, Israel

email: info@mahrwoodpress.com

All of the stories you are about to read are the result of my relationship with Rabbi Dr. David Sholom Pape. He is the main reason for their existence. Our initial meeting occurred almost twenty years ago.

It began with a telephone call. David had gotten my number as a result of his search for a 'Jewish cartoonist.' As editor of the 'Moshiach Times', a magazine produced through the auspices of the Lubavitcher sect of East New York in Brooklyn, he had pursued his search by visiting the offices of a number of comic book publishers. At DC Comics, Paul Levitz, now President and Publisher of DC Comics, suggested he contact me.

So, I got the phone call. I explained to David that my schedule was quite full and I could not take on any additional work. Undeterred, he insisted on wanting to meet and speak to me. So, an appointment was made for a group of Lubavitcher Rabbis, along with David, to drive from Brooklyn to New Jersey, to my home to meet my wife, Muriel and I, and to discuss the possibility of my producing some work for their magazine. They would not, nor could not be dissuaded.

The meeting was fascinating and engrossing. They arrived. Four or five young men, bearded, all wearing black hats and long curly sideburns (payis), black suits, white shirts, no ties. I could see their tzitzis, the fringes of their prayer vestments, when they opened their jackets.

David was first to speak and introduced the others to my wife and myself. With due courtesy, Muriel extended her hand in greeting but was told (with all kindness) that these men were not permitted to even touch a woman's hand.

They had brought mezzuzahs to place on the doorposts of my house, explaining that they contained biblical passages that would protect those who lived within. We thanked them as they proceeded to nail mezzuzahs to the door frames.

Then our discussions proceeded concerning their real purpose for their trip from Brooklyn to the wilds of New Jersey. It went something like this:

"But, David, I have more work than I can handle at this time. I can't—"

"Joe, the busier the man, the more he can do. It needn't be long stories—"

"But, to write and draw even a few pages—"

"But it's a monthly. Only one or two pages."

I could admire their tenacity. So I capitulated. Not really, because they struck a responsive chord in me and I wanted to do it.

My commitment would be limited to two pages a month. David would suggest stories based on biblical references that he felt would be meaningful to his readers. I explained that in order for me to do this work, the stories would have to be meaningful to me as well. It was decided that I would have full freedom to develop and illustrate these stories as I saw fit. We were in agreement, and despite my initial objections to over-loading my schedule, my decision to go ahead was made.

To my own surprise (and pleasure) I was able to maintain producing two pages per month (only missing a few deadlines) for a number of years.

During that time, it was a delight to discuss the stories and their origins with David. We had many discussions concerning the application and validity of the source material, which was both enlightening and educational to me.

My intent was to compose and illustrate stories that would be of interest to contemporary readers. Stories that might impress readers in a modern day world. Stories that would evoke thought and emotion today, based on concepts that have existed for thousands of years.

The characters of Yaakov and Isaac are young Jewish boys with whom the readers could identify.

I feel that the subject matter within these pages is as viable today as they were in biblical times. I wrote and illustrated these stories with those thoughts in mind.

I hope you enjoy them.

JOE KUBERT

1 The Importance of Torah

There, he sat with five young children...and taught each, one book of the Torah...

*...until they knew them **perfectly**... so they could teach others.*

Author's Reflections

Very often we are told that there are certain things expected of us, things we may question but are not fully explained. Students in school are required to read and learn history. Geography and other so-called dry subjects for seemingly little or no reason. They ask, "Why do we have to learn about things we will never use in our daily lives?" And since the Bible was written thousands of years ago, what relevancy does it have today?

This story attempts to answer these questions in a simple, yet dramatic manner.

As with many of the stories in this book, there are references to the fact that these events actually happened. Not made up or imagined, but repeatedly told from generation to generation and scribed by scholars thousands of years ago.

Jews have always felt the pain of persecution and endured the suffering it has caused. In this story, Rabbi Chiya accepts the mission to assure that the tenets that hold his people together will never falter. He does this by demonstrating that the teachings of Torah has a beginning in all things natural.

He raises crops from which he uses fibers to braid rope. The rope is used to trap animals whose hides are used as parchment. The animals' meat is not wasted, but given to those in need of food. With great effort and in time he completes the work of transcribing the five books of the Torah on the dry parchment. Then he takes the important stop of teaching the torah to five young students, who will then each teach another five. The numbers expand continuously, insuring a never-ending chain.

By his deed, the Rabbi has demonstrated the importance of Torah. In varying degrees, these lessons apply to the world today. Perhaps not literally, for the need to raise crops and trap animals is not necessary. But, prevailing hardships must be overcome if the learning is to continue. And learning about the past insures a better future for us all, as Rabbi Chiya has shown.

I DIDN'T EXPECT TO BE *HERE*, ISAAC...IN THE YESHIVAH'S *LIBRARY*... AFTER A DAY OF SCHOOL.

ME NEITHER, YAAKOV. BUT THE TEACHER ASSIGNED US TO GET THE *ALEF - BAIS* BOOKS FOR THE YOUNGER STUDENTS.

I KNOW IT'S IMPORTANT FOR *US* TO LEARN TORAH...BUT--*WHY* DO *WE* HAVE TO TEACH THE LITTLE *KIDS* ALEF - BAIS?

BECAUSE THAT'S WHAT HE *TOLD* US TO DO, YAAKOV.

OOPS! I DROPPED A BOOK.

FUNNY...I NEVER NOTICED THIS BOOK BEFORE.

LOOK, YAAKOV! IT FELL OPEN TO A STORY...

...OF *RABBI CHIYA*...WHO LIVED ALMOST TWO THOUSAND YEARS AGO! IT WAS DURING A TIME WHEN THE JEWISH PEOPLE WERE PERSECUTED...AND THREATENED WITH *EXTINCTION!*

© 1985 JOE KUBERT

YAAKOV AND ISAAC

THE IMPORTANCE OF TORAH

A GREAT SCHOLAR, RABBI CHIYA, *LEFT* HIS STUDIES... ON A MISSION WHOSE PURPOSE *NO ONE COULD UNDERSTAND!*

FIRST, HE PLANTED A FIELD WITH FLAX...

...WHILE EVERYONE WONDERED *WHY* A LEARNED MAN LIKE RABBI CHIYA WOULD CHOOSE TO BECOME A *FARMER!*

THEN, HE WOVE *ROPE NETTING* FROM THE FLAX...

...WITH WHICH HE TRAPPED *DEER*.

WITH THE SKIN OF THE DEER HE MADE *PARCHMENT*...AND GAVE THE MEAT TO THE POOR AND HUNGRY.

IT TOOK HIM MANY, MANY *MONTHS* TO WRITE THE TORAH'S *FIVE BOOKS* ON THE PARCHMENT...

...AND THOSE HE CARRIED TO THE MOST REMOTE VILLAGE HE COULD FIND.

THERE, HE SAT WITH FIVE YOUNG CHILDREN...AND TAUGHT EACH ONE BOOK OF THE TORAH...

...UNTIL THEY KNEW THEM *PERFECTLY*... SO THEY COULD TEACH OTHERS.

AT LAST EVERYONE UNDERSTOOD HOW *GREAT* WAS THE DEED OF RABBI CHIYA... THAT HE MADE SURE THAT THE *TORAH* WOULD *NEVER* BE FORGOTTEN.

BY HIS HARD WORK AND CARE IN *PREPARING* THE TORAH, RABBI CHIYA SHOWS THE IMPORTANCE OF *TEACHING* AND *LEARNING* TORAH.

YES, YAAKOV ...BUT, NOW, WE'D BETTER GET GOING!

OUR STUDENTS WILL BE WAITING FOR US!

The End

At times it seems like history is finally closing its doors on the Jewish people. How can the Jews continue their unique identity and community life after suffering thousands of years of persecutions, dispersions and wandering?

The Jewish people have defied history. They are the only people still in existence and vibrant after 3,500 years of existence. The secret of their existence is the study of Torah. Rabbi Chiya demonstrated this 1900 years ago. During one of the worst periods of persecution that the Jews ever experienced, he didn't throw up his hands in despair. He painstakingly recreated the holy Torah scrolls from the skins of deer he had caught, and began teaching Torah to little children. Those children taught more children and soon many Jews were knowledgeable of the Torah. Once this was accomplished, the Jews' future existence was guaranteed.

Questions to Think About

Q: What is the important lesson in this story?
A: *Its very important for all of us Jews to learn Torah, even the little children. It's the little children who will grow up and spread Torah to others and of course to their children in turn.*

Q: Why did Rabbi Chiya in the story have to become a Farmer?
A: *In those days they didn't have rope at the store. Rabbi Chiya had to make his own rope out of plants. The rope he used to trap deer to he could properly shecht the deer and then use the skin for parchment in order to write a Torah.*

Q: Do we have to work so hard today to write a Torah and to learn Torah?
A: *No, we don't have hard physical, work, but Rabbi Chiya had to do a lot of physical labor to be able to teach torah. Today, we have other obstacles that make it hard for us to learn and teach Torah. For example computer games or other modern technologies and distractions that take us away from Torah and challenge our Yetzer Hora (evil inclinations).*

Q: Can you think of other things that make it hard for us to learn and teach Torah in modern times?

Q: What did Rabbi Chiya achieve by his hard work?

A: *Because of his hard work, he kept the younger children learning torah in hard times. Due to that, we are fortunate to be able to have and learn Torah today. He passed his diligence and love of Torah and learning on down through the generations.*

2 A Helping Hand

Author's Reflections

In the process of doing these stories, I found myself pondering philosophical as well as practical questions. My discussions with Rabbi Dr. David Pape might have sounded more like arguments at times had they been overheard. His references to faith and discipline, at first, gave rise to a cynical reaction from me. I was not prepared, nor was it my desire, to give sugar-coated answers to questions. Over all, I believe the answers should be direct and truthful as possible.

This story involves similar situations many of us, young and old, may face in our lives. To achieve success, how much is dependent on the individual's efforts? How much help should we seek from Hashem? If we do put forth our best efforts, will we receive this help? How much help can we expect? How to answer these questions in two pages?

To begin, I decided to build the story around a sports event; a ten-mile run. Most people can identify with sport competitions. In every contest there are winners and there are losers. I felt that two major elements must be present if one hopes to be a winner.

First, the individual must devote himself to strengthen his abilities. This cannot be done in a haphazard fashion, but in a consistent and disciplined manner. To practice one day and allow two or three days to pass without practicing is as effective as no practice at all. A dedication to a goal must be coupled with great effort and consistency.

Second, the same applies to the matter of faith. That, too, must be consistent and unflagging. After all, He helps those who first help themselves.

So Yaakov has won his race, and Isaac has learned a lesson.

THE RACE BEGINS! FORTY YOUNG RUNNERS START FROM A STANDING POSITION...IGNORING THE COLD, WINTRY CHILL...

RACE COURSE

*E*ACH RUNNER WATCHES FOR AN OPENING...

...THEN...YAAKOV STRIDES AHEAD...

...THE OTHERS CLOSE AT HIS HEELS!

*M*ILE AFTER MILE, THE ATHLETES STRAIN TO OVERTAKE YAAKOV...

...AND AT THE FINISH LINE...

HE'S *WON!*

YAAKOV'S WON THE RACE!

*L*ATER...

YOU *DID* IT, YAAKOV... BUT--WHAT GAVE YOU THAT EXTRA "PUSH" TO WIN?

LOCKE

TOMORROW MORNING...COME TO MY ROOM! I'LL SHOW YOU...

*E*ARLY NEXT MORNING...

YAAKOV...WHAT WERE YOU GOING TO SHOW ME?

THIS ISAAC! PUTTING ON TEFILLIN EVERY MORNING TAUGHT ME THE MEANING OF *DISCIPLINE*... AND BEING *TRULY* PREPARED!

I TRIED MY BEST...THEN I *KNEW* I *COULD* WIN WITH THE HELP OF HASHEM!

The End

Judaism makes many demands from its adherents. Jews have to rigorously keep dozens and even hundreds of mitzvahs every day. This training teaches a Jew to live a disciplined life. An observant Jew is better able to cope with life challenges because Jewish law has taught him internal discipline. It will even affect how well he does in a race! A Jew puts on his tefillin each morning because it is a commandment from Hashem to do so. A basic tenet of the Jewish faith is that everything Hashem does or commands is only good. It is easy to see how keeping the Mitzvah of tefillin has the additional benefit of laying a groundwork of discipline for Yaakov that helped him to prepare and win his race. Even if you're disciplined by keeping mitzvos, it's no guarantee that you'll win a race. Discipline is only one factor towards success.

Questions to Think About

Q: According to the story, how should a person prepare himself to be successful in life?
A: *A person should be disciplined, try his hardest and ask Hashem to help him as well.*

Q: What is the race in the story compared to in real life?
A: *Real life itself is a race. Anything worthwhile that a person wants to accomplish is difficult, but can be achieved with effort and persistance. Our Sages tell us that Hashem will help us along the right path in life, but we must make the effort to set out on that path with all its obstacles. Living a good Jewish life is like running in the race and succeeding.*

Q: What did Yaakov mean when he said that putting on his tefillin makes him disciplined?
A: *Having to get up very early in the morning and putting on tefillin everyday (or just getting up to daven if you are not Bar mitzvah) helps a person to become accustomed to being regular and systematic and in control of himself. Thus he is able to be organized and accomplish a lot. It also accustoms a person to connecting with Hashem, so that not only does a person help himself, but Hashem becomes a strong part of his life and helps him also.*

Thought Question

Q: What are your goals in life? How can you help yourself achieve them? How can you make Hashem a greater part of you life?

3 A Matter of Importance

IN YAAKOV'S MIND, THE *ALTER REBBE* WALKS TOWARD A COTTAGE ON THE OUTSKIRTS OF TOWN...

Author's Reflections

When does religious ritual become less important, secondary in the scheme of life? I believe this simple story answers that complex question.

The 'Alter Rebbe' (Rabbi Shneur Zalman of Liadi) looks very much as I remember my grandfather, white bearded, a look of seriousness in his steady gaze. I had attended synagogue on the high holy days, with both my father and my grandfather. This was in East New York, in Brooklyn, many, many years ago. The synagogue was actually a small, vacant store on Sutter Avenue converted for its current use by the insertion of a small, rude ark in which rested the Torah. Perhaps twenty or twenty-five people crowded into the small space. I can still smell the dust, the tabac which my grandfather would give me to sniff. "It will clear your nose," he said. The quiet was pervasive, broken only by softly intoned words of those in prayer.

Yom Kippur, the day of atonement, when we ask forgiveness of past sins, is the holiest of holy days. Even those who rarely attend synagogue would not miss that day. Yet, this story describes a situation where it is permissible—even necessary—not to attend, and one may even leave if services are actually in progress. To have a rabbi leave the Yom Kippur services demonstrates the importance of the situation. How did the rabbi learn of the sick woman's condition? Did someone tell him, or did it come to him in a vision? In either case, the important thing was to answer the call.

The lesson teaches us is that no matter how involved we are, how important we think our own work or thoughts, there are other things that are more important. A loved one who needs you. Someone who is ill and needs help, or even a stranger in trouble. People are of importance and supercede all else. We must put things in proper order in our lives and have a clear understanding in terms of their importance.

THE YEAR: LATE 1700'S... THE PLACE: A VILLAGE IN EAST RUSSIA... THE DAY: *YOM KIPPUR!*

AN ASTONISHED GASP RISES FROM THE CONGREGATION, AS THE *ALTER REBBE* REMOVES HIS TALLIS...

...AND LEAVES THE SHUL *BEFORE THE SERVICE IS OVER!*

NOW, LET US COME TO THE *PRESENT*...IN THE HOME OF *YAAKOV* AND *ISAAC*...WHERE THEY SPEAK OF...

A MATTER OF IMPORTANCE!

I'M TAKING *MATZAH* FOR *PEACH* TO SOME OLD AND SICK PEOPLE, YAAKOV...

LEAVE YOUR STUDIES FOR AWHILE AND COME WITH ME.

I'D *LIKE* TO, ISAAC...BUT... I *MUST* FINISH STUDYING THIS CHAPTER!

AS HE SPEAKS, A *VISION* SUDDENLY FILLS YAAKOV'S MIND...

© 1985 JOE KUBERT

IN YAAKOV'S MIND, THE *ALTER REBBE* WALKS TOWARD A COTTAGE ON THE OUTSKIRTS OF TOWN...

HE CHOPS WOOD...

...MAKES SOUP

...AND TENDERLY FEEDS THE SICK WOMAN WHO LIVES IN THE COTTAGE.

ONLY THEN DOES THE *ALTER REBBE* RETURN TO SHUL...TO FINISH THE PRAYERS FOR *YOM KIPPUR*!

WAIT A MINUTE ISAAC... I'M GOING **WITH** YOU!

HUH? OKAY, YAAKOV...THAT'S **GREAT**!

THEIR GIFTS OF MATZAH... AND THEIR JOY IN *GIVING*... SENDS WAVES OF HAPPINESS INTO GRATEFUL HEARTS.

TELL ME YAAKOV... *WHY* DID YOU DECIDE TO COME WITH ME?

The End

YOU REMINDED ME OF AM *IMPORTANT LESSON*, ISAAC...

THE FIRST RABBI OF LUBAVITCH...THE *ALTER REBBE*... PUT *EVERY-THING* ASIDE, IN ORDER TO HELP SOMEONE WHOSE LIFE WAS IN DANGER. HE COULD HAVE SENT SOMEONE *ELSE*... BUT IT WAS *TOO IMPORTANT*... *HE* HAD TO DO IT *HIMSELF*!

NOW *I* CAN GO BACK TO *MY* STUDIES!

Assisting others in need is the most important deed a person can do, especially when there is no one else who can do it. The Alter Rebbe left his holy prayers to chop wood, to cook a meal and feed a lonely sick woman, because G-d prefers our lovingkindness to our fellow humans more than our prayers.

It must be added that when at all possible, such decisions must be made by a proper Rabbi and a mature individual who can weigh the needs of the moment.

The Talmud teaches us that he who saves one life is as if he saved an entire world. Imagine the awesome responsibility of protecting and preserving life. One life equals a world, including each of our own lives. We must take care to protect ourselves and our health and well being as much as we look out for others.

Questions to Think About

Q: What is the important lesson we can learn in this story?
A: *Sometimes no matter how important we think our own work or thoughts may be (even our Torah learning!). Other things might be more important, like doing a certain Mitzvah, for example helping a sick person.*

Q: Why did the Alter Rebbe in the story leave Shule on Yom Kippur, the holiest day of the year?
A: *He had to go feed a sick woman who would have died had he not helped her. This was more important.*

Q: Why did Yaakov change his mind about going with Isaac?
A: *He remembered the famous story about the Alter Rebbe.*

Q: What does the Torah say about this kind of situation?
A: *Helping a sick person takes priority.*

Thought Question

Q: Did you ever have an important decision to make between two important Mitzvahs? Which one did you choose and why? Do you think that you made the right decision?

4 The Kutim

Author's Reflections

I confess that the background for this story was completely new to me. This is part of the education I experienced at the hands of Rabbi Dr. David Pape, for which I will always be grateful.

There are historical references for this story, based on an occurrence which took place during the time of Alexander the Great. It exemplifies the fact that Jews have been used as a scapegoat throughout the ages. For contemporary readers, it helps gain a perspective on both that which occurred thousands of years ago and events that are happening in the world today.

Those who wish to gain power or favor, like the Kutim, will use any device to do so. Even if it means lying, cheating or bringing harm to innocents.

"Look, they have so much money. They control everything."

"You are poor and they are rich."

"They think they are so smart."

"They wish to do you harm."

Alexander was taunted by the Kutim to deal harshly with the Jews. But Alexander was wise beyond his years and recognized the honesty of the Jewish priests and listened to their pleas for justice. The priests did not hide the fact they were Jews in their manner or dress, which gained them the respect of Alexander.

My intention in doing this story was to make the characters of Alexander, the Kutim and the priests as credible as possible. If the characters are believable, then the story will be effective and meaningful.

THE KUTIM

YOU *MUST* LISTEN TO US ALEXANDER ...OR ELSE *THOSE PEOPLE* WILL UNDER-MINE YOUR RULE! THEY ARE *REBELLIOUS*-

WE ARE THE *TRUE* BELIEVERS... *THEY* PLOT *AGAINST* YOU!

HMM... WHAT DO YOU *KUTIM* SUGGEST I DO?

I WILL CONSIDER IT! BUT FIRST...

...I WILL SPEAK TO THEIR PRIEST, *SHIMON HATZADIK!*

DESTROY THEIR TEMPLE...THE BAIS HAMIKDOSH!

THEY WILL BE HUMBLED ...IF THEIR *TEMPLE* IS *NO MORE!*

*I*N THE TIME OF THE *BAIS HAMIK-DOSH* , A GROUP CALLED THE *KUTIM* TRIED TO TURN *ALEXANDER THE GREAT* -- WHOSE POWER EXTENDED OVER THE *HOLY LAND* -- AGAINST THE JEWS!

© 1985 JOE KUBERT

WORD IS SENT TO THE *BAIS HAMIKDOSH*...ALEXANDER DEMANDS THAT *SHIMON* MUST APPEAR BEFORE HIM!

IT IS THE *KUTIM* WHO SEEK POWER... BY USING *US* AS A *SCAPEGOAT* SHIMON!

YES...WE MUST PRAY TO HASHEM...TO HELP US CONVINCE ALEXANDER OF THAT FACT!

*T*HAT NIGHT, THE COHANIM-PRIESTS STARTED FOR *ALEXANDER'S* ENCAMPMENT...

...UNDER THE EVIL EYES OF THE *KUTIM*!

LOOK-- SHIMON WEARS HIS PRIESTLY VESTMENTS! ALEXANDER WILL THINK THIS A *BOASTING* OF POWER!

YES...AND THEIR *BAIS HAMIKDOSH* WILL BE *DESTROYED*!

*A*T DAWN...

WE HAVE COME TO SHOW HONOR AND RESPECT...

WAIT! YOUR ROBES...YOUR FACE...

I HAVE SEEN YOU... *BEFORE-*

"...IN ALL MY BATTLES, A *VISION* STOOD BESIDE ME...*ENCOURAGED* ME... STRENGTHENED MY HEART!"

THE VISION... WAS OF YOU SHIMON HA-TZADIK!

FEAR NOT, SHIMON... YOU AND YOUR PEOPLE WILL *ALWAYS* HAVE MY FAVOR...AS I HAVE YOURS! AND THOSE WHO WISH YOU HARM... WILL *THEMSELVES* SUFFER!

≡PHEW≡! SHIMON RISKED HIS LIFE...GOING TO ALEXANDER IN THE *GARMENTS* OF THE *HIGH PRIEST*, YAAKOV!

YES, ISAAC! AND *THAT* IS WHY HE WON ALEXANDER'S *RESPECT* AND SAVED THE *BAIS HA MIKDOSH.*

The End

The Kutim were a group of non-Jews who had been transferred to the Land of Israel by their Babylonian conqueror. They partially kept Judaism, but saw the Jews as rivals and tried to obstruct their every move after the Jews returned from Babylonia.

When Alexander of Macedonia arrived as victor in Jerusalem, the Kutim saw their opportunity to defame the Jews. They warned him that the Jews were rebels who would revolt against him.

The Jews were in great danger because of the slander, but the Chief Priest, Shimon, bravely decided to meet with Alexander at the head of a distinguished entourage to demonstrate his allegiance. Because the Jews were deserving, G-d helped them. When Alexander saw Shimon, he realized that his vision appeared to him before his victories, and he rejected the Kutim's accusations.

There will always be people who are jealous and wish one evil. But a person needn't worry about them if he lives his life as he should. Hashem will always be at his side helping him in original, unexpected ways.

Questions to Think About

Q: What were the Kutim trying to do?
A: They were trying to make Alexander destroy the Jewish People. They were telling lies about the Jews. They were seeking power for themselves and using the Jews as scapegoats.

Q: What did Alexander do? Did he listen to those people?
A: No, he decided to speak to the Jewish High Priest - Shimon HaTzaddik.

Q: Why did Shimon Hatzaddik dress in his priestly garments?
A: He davened to Hashem, therefore Hashem inspired him to go to Alexander wearing the priestly garments, to show honor to the king. We should always ask Hashem to help us with our problems.

Q: What miracle happened that made Shimon Hatzaddik help save the Jews from Alexander and the Kuttim?
A: Hashem made Shimon Hatzaddik's image appear before Alexander in his battles and dreams encouraging him and helping him. Thus, Alexander recognized Shimon Hatzaddik when he came to him in person.

5 An Act of Resistance

AT THE HEIGHT OF *WORLD WAR II*, POLISH JEWS WERE FORCED INTO THE *WARSAW GHETTO!* THIS WAS THE LAST STOP BEFORE THE CONCENTRATION CAMPS...AND THE OVENS! STARVING...WITH LITTLE MEANS OF DEFENSE... THE JEWS FACED THEIR OPPRESSORS!

Author's Reflections

One of the more important causes for the second World War was Hitler's intention for the complete annihilation of the Jewish people. This is called genocide, the act of killing a people by means of the planned murder of men, women and children. The toll of six million Jewish lives reflects how close Hitler came to achieving his goal. This story tells why he could never succeed.

The uprising in the Warsaw Ghetto in April of 1943 must and will be told over and over again. How a small vestige of young Jewish survivors fought side by side against the Nazi horde despite the knowledge that their deaths were inevitable. They fought against tanks and cannons, were outnumbered by an army of thousands, and finally chased from building to burning building into the cellars and sewers below, only to be cornered and killed. This truly was a supreme "Act of Resistance".

But, another important aspect of this story is the continued faith displayed under extraordinary circumstances. I attempted to show the relevancy between the reaction of people today as compared to those trapped in the purgatory of the Warsaw Ghetto. Today, principles and practices of one's faith are at times put aside for any number of reasons; a ball game, a movie, watching TV or logging in online with a friend. We forget the deprivation and cruelty people have endured, who despite it all adhered to their beliefs. In the midst of carnage, children attended cheder, Hebrew school. Think about it for a minute. People held in the Warsaw Ghetto knew that the Nazis intended to kill them all, men, women and children. No one would survive. Yet, they continued to teach the children Torah. Above all else, parents believed the children must learn Torah. How else would the heritage survive? And the heritage does survive.

It is a lesson sharply etched in blood. The enemy could not understand how these unarmed Jews could withstand such an onslaught. As the character in the story expressed, "...learning Torah is our supreme act of resistance."

YOU JEWS... STAND AGAINST THE WALL!

PUT THEM WITH THE OTHERS FOR *TRANSIT!*

THESE JEWS *AMAZE* ME! HOW CAN THEY RESIST FOR SO LONG...WITH SO *LITTLE?*

"WE *BURN* THE BUILDINGS... BUT, THEY STILL CLING BY THEIR BLOODY FINGERTIPS! WHAT IS THE *SECRET* OF THEIR *STRENGTH?*"

IN A DARK CORNER OF THE GHETTO, IN AN OLD CRUMBLING BUILDING...

SHH, CHAIM... SOMEONE IS AT THE DOOR!

IT MUST BE MOISHE!

CALMLY, NOW YUSSELE... WE STUDY *BERAISHIS.* SHMUL WILL HELP YOU FOLLOW AS I READ.

L-LET ME IN HURRY!

YES... YES...

CHAIM...THE NAZIS ARE MAKING A HOUSE-TO-HOUSE SEARCH!

WE MUST JOIN THE OTHERS-

YES-- BUT, FOR THE MOMENT --THERE IS *TIME,* MOISHE.

AND WHILE WE HAVE THE TIME, WE MUST TEACH THE CHILDREN *TORAH!*

IN THE TORAH IS OUR STRENGTH...AND THE CHILDREN LEARNING TORAH IS OUR *SUPREME ACT* OF *RESISTANCE!*

THE NAZIS TRIED TO ANNIHILATE THE GHETTO TO CELEBRATE HITLER'S BIRTHDAY.

THEY DID *NOT SUCCEED!* THE JEWS HELD OUT... EVEN LONGER THAN *POLAND!*

I UNDER-STAND, YAAKOV. PLAYING BALL *IS* IMPORTANT...BUT LEARNING TORAH IS THE *SOURCE* OF OUR *HERITAGE!*

THAT IS A LESSON WE MUST *NEVER* FORGET!

The End

Fighting enemies is a courageous act of resistance. But, an even greater act of resistance is living according to one's beliefs and maintaining one's devotion to G-d even during the most harrowing times. Despite starvation, persecution, and uncertainty of the future, Jews in the Warsaw Ghetto pursued the study of Torah even though they knew they were endangering themselves.

The Jews have suffered from countless persecutions, exiles and sufferings, but our devotion to G-d has enabled us to survive down until today.

The Polish buckled under to the Nazi attack in short order to save themselves from further destruction. The Nazis took their time to destroy every building in the Warsaw ghetto to insure that not one Jew remained alive.

The Jews now faced with certain physical destruction, fought back with a ferocity that startled the Nazis. Rabbi Menachem Ziemba, the famed Rabbi of Warsaw became the single most important moral force in the ghetto. In the darkest days of the ghetto, he strove to bring a note of optimism and hope into the lives of the people. He constantly railed against those who seemed to be lost in despair.

He set up secret places for the study of Torah - yeshivas, Talmud Torahs and Bais Yaakovs. At great personal risk, he would constantly visit these holy places in cellars, attics or bomb shelters in order to strengthen those who studied there. He was given two opportunities to escape from the ghetto, but stayed and was murdered by the Nazis. He epitomized the story Yaakov told Isaac and stands as a model for us all.

Questions to Think About

Q: Why was it important for Isaac to stop playing ball when his brother called him?
A: *He needed to go to yeshiva, which was extremely important for him as a Jew, to learn Torah. Without Torah the Jewish people cannot endure.*

Q: Why did Yaakov use the example of the Warsaw Ghetto to help his brother understand the importance of Learning Torah?
A: *Even when the Jewish People were suffering so greatly in World War II in the Warsaw Ghetto, they still made time to learn Torah. Without Torah learning the Jewish People cannot exist, so this was how they resisted their enemies. How much more so should we learn Torah when we're not suffering from war.*

Q: Hitler's goal during the second world war was the complete and total physical and spiritual annihilation of the Jewish people. Even though six million people were killed in WWII, why didn't Hitler succeed in achieving his goal?
A: *Hashem has always promised that he will never completely forsake the Jewish people. Also, the Jews have always had a strong determination to learn Torah and continue their heritage no matter what. After WWII, the surviving Rabbis and scholars reestablished Yeshivas in America, Israel, and other places, and began the process of restoring what was destroyed in Europe. They succeeded. Today there are more Yeshivahs and Torah learning than at any time since the days of the Second Temple! Anyone can grab the opportunity to learn at any time, and in relative peace and quiet and security. It is a wonderful time to be Jewish and learn Torah.*

Thought Question

Q: How can you help to keep your Jewish Heritage?

6 The Jewish Heart

Author's Reflections

How important is it to help someone in trouble?

This simple story answers that question on many levels. What if the person who is in trouble is someone whom you don't like? If you are the one in trouble, what would you think of someone who didn't help you? What if the situation was a matter of life or death?

This is quite a number of complex questions upon which to shed some light within two pages of pictures and words.

As in all the stories in this book, both Rabbi Dr. David Pape and I tried to be as honest and forthright as we could be.

When Isaac drops his groceries and becomes angry at Arnie for not helping him, who can blame Isaac for his reaction? Wouldn't that anger you? But a lesson is learned (taught?), when Yaakov remarks that understanding is more constructive than anger. We can learn from the mistakes and errors in judgement of others. And under all circumstances, one's relationship to a fellow Jew is most important.

The story that happened in the first World War might be apocryphal, but it's said to be true. It could have happened anywhere, at any time, under similar life-threatening conditions. But, to me, the point goes even deeper. If you should not harm a fellow Jew, even in war, why should anyone harm another human? To secure one's own safety, yes. To stop pain and violence visited on loved ones, yes. To protect the weak and helpless, yes. These are actions of self-preservation and protection, not mindless violence.

When one Jewish soldier voices part of a prayer: Sh-Sh'ma Yisroel... Hashem Elokainu Hashem Echod (English translation: Hear, O Israel: The L-rd our G-d, The L-rd is One), it is answered by his opposition, another Jewish soldier: Baruch Shem Kevod... Malchuso L'olum Vo'ed (English translation: Blessed is the Name of his glorious kingdom for all eternity). This is enough to tell them both that they could never be enemies.

If we can practice the underlying thoughts and tenets described in this story, perhaps we can all benefit by having a "Jewish heart".

"THE EXPLOSIONS STOP...THE SILENCE IS DEAFENING..."

HERE... THEY... COME...

"THE ENEMY CHARGES THROUGH THE SMOKE AND FUMES..."

"THE SOLDIERS LOCK IN DEADLY HAND-TO-HAND COMBAT... "

"THE FRENCH SOLDIER FALLS BACKWARD... A STEEL BAYONET IS RAISED TO KILL ..."

SH-SH'MA YISROEL... HASHEM ELOKEINU HASHEM ECHOD!

"THE JEW'S PRAYER IS ANSWERED!"

BARUCH SHEM KEVOD MALCHUSO L'OLAM VO'ED!

"IN THE MIDDLE OF A WAR, TWO JEWS STOP FIGHTING ...AND ARE FRIENDS!"

YOU SEE, ISAAC, IN SPITE OF EVERYTHING A JEW MUST HAVE LOVE FOR HIS FELLOW JEW!

LOOK YAKOV... HERE COMES ARNIE!

I'M SORRY, ISAAC... I WAS WRONG TO LAUGH AT YOU! LET ME HELP YOU CARRY YOUR BUNDLES!

THANK YOU, ARNIE... YAAKOV MADE A POINT THAT YOU JUST PROVED!

The End

27

The unity and closeness which Jews feel towards each other is unlike anything that other coreligionists feel for each other. While a Christian living in the U.S. may feel no special sentiment for a Christian in Nigeria or Thailand, Jews deeply care about the welfare of their brothers wherever they are in the world.

That is also why there are so many Jewish charity organizations which build Jewish hospitals, offer social services for Jews, create Jewish educational institutions, and help Jewish immigrants and the poor.

This special tie between Jews exists because of the unique covenant which Avraham made with G-d. Avraham longed for his descendants to fulfill G-d's commandments and be a holy nation, and G-d promised that they would be His special people from all peoples on the earth. Jews are an organic whole.

Unfortunately, it is not very often in the real world that someone like Arnie would have a change of heart. This is certainly something that we can all strive for.

Questions to Think About

Q: Why did Isaac become angry at Arnie?
A: *Arnie wouldn't stop and help him and he was laughing at him as well.*

Q: Did anything like this ever happen to you? What do you think you would do?

Q: What happens if the person in trouble is someone you don't like? Should you help him anyway?
A: *Yes, you should always try and help people unless it is someone who is very wicked.*

Q: Why did Yaakov use the war story to teach Isaac to love his fellow Jew?
A: *Even though the men were fighting in a war against each other they still did the mitzvah of loving a fellow jew.*

Q: Why do you think Arnie came back to help Isaac after all?
A: *He probably felt bad that he was so mean to Isaac.*

Q: What is the big lesson we learn from this story?
A: *No matter what you should always try and love your fellow Jews and never speak loshon horah about a fellow Jew.*

7 Walking the Tightrope

"...UNTIL, FINALLY...
HE MADE IT SAFELY TO
THE OTHER SIDE."

Author's Reflections

The wise man says you can learn a great deal from paying attention to the most commonplace things that happen all around you. Certainly, great books contain much knowledge and we should learn from past wisdom. Yet, even the most commonplace acts can teach us important lessons from which we can benefit.

A watchmaker works with meticulous attention on a broken clock. He peers through a magnifying glass to correct the intricate and delicate mechanisms. His concentration is completely centered on his work. His patience is unending.

What wonderful works each of us could accomplish if we apply the watchmaker's diligence.

Olympic athletes devote themselves to physical fitness. They exercise for hours each day to prepare for their competitions. Their accomplishments are the results of years of constant practice. Their total dedication to be the best is a lesson for us all. If we apply this single-mindedness to whatever our goal, we can accomplish it.

In our story, the tightrope performer executes a death-defying act by walking across a thin wire over a deep precipice. He has practiced this acrobatic feat for a long time, only a few feet off the ground. He has probably fallen many times before gaining the ability of perfect balance. Still, he takes a chance with his life. One slip and it is all over. But, he has learned his art well and is rewarded with success.

If we slip, the results can be painful, but not catastrophic. By preparing ourselves, by learning from the past and present, we can lessen the possibilities of failure.

WALKING A TIGHTROPE

K. JOE KUBERT © 1990

LOOK AT *THAT*, ZEIDI ONE SLIP AND HE'S A *GONER!*

CIRCUS

SEE THESE DEATH-DEFYING AERIAL...ANZAS

I WOULDN'T DO IT FOR *ALL THE MONEY IN THE WORLD!*

EXCITING, ISAAC? I IMAGINE IT IS... I REMEMBER THE FIRST TIME I EVER SAW A TIGHTROPE WALKER... IT WAS A LONG, LONG TIME AGO...

IT'S *SCAREY...*

...BUT... IT LOOKS *EXCITING!*

"I WAS THE SAME AGE AS YOU AND YAAKOV, ISAAC ...IT WAS IN THE SMALL VILLAGE WHERE I WAS BORN. EVERYONE CAME TO WATCH THE DARING PERFORMANCE."

"MY HEART WAS BEATING WILDLY AS THE MAN BALANCED ON THIN WIRE HIGH OVER OUR HEADS..."

"ONE MIS-STEP WOULD COST HIS LIFE."

Life is a tightrope walk. The sage, Rabbi Nachman of Breslav, would say, "The world is a very narrow bridge, and the main thing to remember is not to be afraid!"

Everyone has his trials and ordeals in life. Sometimes the going gets scary. But as long as we are focused on the right values and goals, and strive to live a life faithful to Torah, we will pass our trials successfully -- just as the tightrope walker doesn't fall because he keeps his eyes on the end of the line.

Questions to Think About

Q: What did Yaakov and Isaac see at the circus that was exciting and scarey?
A: A Tight rope walker

Q: Why do you think this man would do something so dangerous for a living?
A: He wants to have excitement or maybe to earn a lot of money or to become famous.

Q: Why did Zeidi's father take him to see the tightrope walker when he was a little boy?
A: He believed that we can learn a lot from this man.

Q: What can we learn from the tightrope walker?
A: We should never risk our lives as this man does for fame and fortune. We need to concentrate on every step of our lives to make sure that we do the right thing and stick to Torah and mitzvahs only.

Q: Why did Zeidi's father compare the lives of the Jewish people to a tight rope walker?
A: We need to concentrate and only do Torah and Mitzvahs to succeed and receive our reward. Sometimes it is very hard to keep the Mitzvahs. But, as Rabbi Akiva said, "If it is difficult to be a fish in the water, how much more difficult is it to live as a fish out of the water?"

Thought Question

Q: Were you ever In a situation where it was very hard to keep the Torah and Mitzvahs?

Q: What happened?

Q: In the end did you succeed?

8 Up Or Down

Author's Reflections

I think that almost everyone has faced a situation when we had convinced ourselves that the outcome was going to be a bad one. One in which we felt we were a sure loser even before the results were in. The odds seemed so much against our ending up, we were certain we'd end down. We were going to lose. There was no chance of succeeding. So why even try?

In this story, Isaac knew he'd strike out, so he did. He had put his own conclusion on his efforts before he'd even tried. And because he thought he couldn't succeed, his attempt was only half-hearted. In the end, he fulfilled his own prediction.

Every day we face problems in our lives. They arise in school, business and at home. We cannot allow them to overwhelm us or beat us down.

It simply takes the pleasure out of living.

It's important to maintain a "can do" attitude, regardless of the problems we face. If not, we're beaten before we start. Any athlete will tell you that attitude is a major part of what it takes to win. If you feel your opponent is superior and will beat you, you've already lost. If your schoolwork is tough and you say, "I can't do it.", then you've already resigned from trying and you won't do it.

A positive or "up" attitude can save your life. There are many true stories of soldiers in the heat of battle who have survived simply because they refused to go "down". By all odds they should have been beaten, defeated. Instead, they fought on. They didn't give in.

We must always look "up".

YAAKOV and ISAAC

UP... OR DOWN

STRIKE THREE... YOU'RE **OUT!**

I-I **KNEW** I'D STRIKE OUT. I'M JUST NOT AS GOOD A PLAYER AS THE OTHERS.

JOE KUBERT
© 1993

Later, YAAKOV AND ISAAC HEAD FOR HOME...

I JUST **KNEW** I WAS GOING TO MISS THAT LAST PITCH, YAAKOV.

IT HAPPENS. **EVERYONE** MISSES ONCE IN A WHILE.

YOU'VE **GOT** TO THINK **POSITIVELY.**

1

YEAH... SURE. FORGET IT.

SURE. LET'S TAKE THE CLIFF TRAIL.

LET'S GO HOME THROUGH THE PARK O.K.?

GEE...IT'S **BEAUTIFUL** HERE ON "LOOKOUT POINT".

YES, ISAAC. HASHEM HAS MADE THIS WORLD A WONDERFUL PLACE TO--

YAAKOV-- GRAB ME!

I'M... **SLIPPING!**

HANG ON, ISAAC... HANG ON! I'LL GO FOR HELP-

NO! I-I'M *SLIPPING* D-DON'T... LEAVE ME... YAAKOV...

I-I'M *SCARED* I...CAN'T HOLD ON. IT'S...NO USE-

STAY *COOL* ISAAC... *DON'T GIVE UP!* I'M WITH YOU...AND SO IS -

I - I KNOW.

SHEMA YISROEL HASHEM ELOKAINU HASHEM ECHOD.

THAT'S IT, ISAAC. GOOD. NOW-- PUT IT IN YOUR MIND THAT YOU *CAN* MAKE IT!

THINK THAT YOU'RE *CLIMBING UP!* THAT'S THE STUFF ...YOU *ARE* CLIMBING UP...

UNH... OOMPH. IT-IT'S *TOUGH* YAAKOV!

SURE IT'S TOUGH... BUT...YOU CAN *DO* IT...

I-I *MADE* IT! YAAKOV...I'M ON THE LEDGE. I'M GOING TO BE O.K.!

I'M *UP*, YAAKOV! I - I DIDN'T THINK I COULD DO IT...BUT... I *DID!*

ONCE YOU STARTED TO THINK *POSITIVELY*, EVERYTHING CHANGED.

THINKING GOOD *CAN MAKE* IT *GOOD!* THANKS TO *YOU*... AND *HASHEM!*

End

Positive thinking can make the difference between a life of success or failure. Everyone has setbacks and emergencies that seem insurmountable. But, with willpower, belief in oneself, and trust in G-d, a person is often able to extricate himself from seemingly impossible situations.

Call on Hashem because He is ever-present, He listens to us, and no one can help like Him!

Positive thinking is not an cure-all for everything, including falling off a cliff. Vigilence, dedication and perseverence all go a long way in helping a person succeed in life's challenges.

Questions to Think About

Q: Why was Isaac so upset about the baseball game?
A: *He struck out, and he was as good as the other players, or could become as good as the other players.*

Q: What was Yaakov trying to tell Isaac about the ball game?
A: *You have to think positively about things in life and try your best.*

Q: When Isaac fell off the cliff what happened to him? Was he thinking positively?
A: *No, not at all. He thought he was going to fall all the way down. He thought he wouldn't make it.*

Q: How did Yaakov help Isaac?
A: *He helped him by staying with him and encouraging him to think positively.*

Q: What dilemma did Yaakov face in this story?
A: *He might have run away and left Isaac to try to get help. By staying he was able to offer encouragement and if needed he might have figured a different way to help Isaac.*

Q: Why does thinking positively help you do things you don't think you can do?
A: *If you tell your mind that "you can do it" you usually can. If you tell yourself you can't do it, then you usually can't. The mind is a very positive tool Hashem gave us to use but we must make sure we "think positively".*

9 | Into The Shadows

Author's Reflections

This story was written and drawn twenty years ago, but it is as current today as it has been over the thousands of years under which Jews all over the world have suffered and survived.

All though history, anti-Semitism has caused Jewish anguish and death. One only needs to scan the history books of the World War that started in the 1940s. Of kristallnacht in 1938. Of the concentration camps and the annihilation of six million Jewish men, women and children.

Is it any wonder that fear has crept into the hearts of many? That some would try to hide the fact that they are Jews?

This story tells us that we must not be afraid when we find ourselves in strange or unfamiliar surroundings. Not to be belligerent or confrontational, but neither should we be fearful or try to hide the fact that we are Jews.

After lengthy discussions with Rabbi Dr. David Pape, I felt this story should be told simply and with a minimum of graphic violence. It's effectiveness should be in what is not said, what is not described visually, but is only intimated.

The difficulty was limiting it to only two pages.

The point being made was not that Yaakov and Isaac were acting in a 'bravado' manner in the face of probable danger, but they would not be ashamed of the fact they were Jews. Rather, that they would face the situation squarely and answer taunts calmly and rationally.

We must all remember, however, that there are no guarantees in life. We must be prepared to face the consequences of situations with honesty and our best efforts.

INTO THE SHADOWS

Y-YAAKOV... I-UH-THINK WE TOOK A *WRONG TURN!*

YES, ISAAC...WE'VE NEVER BEEN IN *THIS* PART OF THE CITY BEFORE!

HEY! LOOKIT *THEM*, WILLYA?

WHERE'D *THEY* COME FROM?

MARS?

FUNNY-LOOKIN *STUFF* THEY'RE WEARIN' ...A *BEANIE* AN' *STRINGS!*

LOOKS LIKE *TROUBLE* YAAKOV! M-MAYBE WE SHOULD *HIDE* OUR YARMULKAS AND TZI-TZIS, SO...

NO!

"WE SHOULD *NEVER* TRY TO HIDE THE FACT THAT WE ARE *JEWS*...EVEN IF IT COULD MEAN *DANGER!*"

© 1984 JOE KUBERT

WHEN THE *NAZIS* CAME INTO POWER, THEIR INTENTION WAS TO *ELIMINATE* US!

EVERY *JEW!*

"SOME PEOPLE TRIED TO HIDE THE FACT THEY WERE JEWS--BUT--IT DIDN'T HELP THEM!"

"PEOPLE WERE ARRESTED... THEIR BUSINESSES *DESTROYED*... SIMPLY BECAUSE THEY WERE JEWS!"

"CONCENTRATION CAMPS WERE *FILLED* WITH MEN WOMEN AND CHILDREN! SIX MILLION, ISAAC...*SIX MILLION!*

NO! WE WILL *NOT* HIDE OUR JEWISHNESS!

COME ON ISAAC!

HEY... WHAT KINDA *HATS* YOU GOT ON?

WE ARE *JEWS*... AND THESE "BEANIES" SIGNIFY THAT G-D IS *ALWAYS* WITH US!

AND THESE ARE *TZITZIS*...TO REMIND US OF *HIS* COMMANDMENTS THAT WE FOLLOW!

HEY...THAT'S *NEAT.* THEM FRINGES!

YEAH! YOU GUYS ARE *O.K.!*

SEE YOU AROUND!

*L*ATER...

W-WE WERE *LUCKY*, YAAKOV...

WE MUST *NEVER* HIDE THAT WE ARE *JEWS!* THE PRICE OF *FEAR* IS TOO MUCH FOR *ANY* OF US TO PAY!

The End

39

It's not always easy to appear Jewish. Jews have always been targeted by bullies and oppressors, and appearing in Jewish dress sometimes invites trouble.

Nevertheless, a Jew is proud of his kipa and tzitzis, which shows that he is a servant of Hashem. We know that in the merit of our ancestors in Egypt refusing to change their Jewish clothing, Hashem saved them. Even if we sometimes have to pay a price for appearing different, we will never give up our Jewish clothes which show our special connection to Hashem.

The world has changed and turned into a more dangerous place in the twenty years since this story was written. In today's world, real hoodlums may well see the Jewish kids and not be impressed that they are wearing beanies and tzitzis because "Hashem is with us." They'd say something instead like "Let's beat them up and see if Hashem is still with them."

Yaakov's conclusion: "We must never hide that we are Jews. The price of fear is too much for any of us to pay", is admirable but must also be weighed and measured. The Jewish imperative is to survive, and if one has to hide his overt signs of Judaism to survive, then that can sometimes be a correct strategy. Never hiding one's Judaism despite knowing it will incite anti-Semites nearby is a bad strategy, and will only increase fear. When faced with possible public pogroms, Rabbi Sitruk, the Chief Rabbi of France, told Jews in France not to wear a kipa but only a regular hat to protect themselves.

Hashem gave us the Torah to live by. One of the commandments given in the Torah is that of following the words of the Rabbis in each generation. What worked and was proper for one generation may be the exact opposite of that which is proper in another generation. While Rabbis are not always available in every given situation, as often as we can, we must consult with them to determine what it is Hashem wants of us and so guide our lives.

Questions to Think About

Q: How did you think Yaakov and Isaac felt as they approached the street gang?
A: *They were scared that they may get hurt and teased because they were outnumbered and they were Jewish.*

Q: Why did Isaac want to hide his Yarmulka and Tzitzis when they approached the street gang?
A: *Isaac was worried that they would get teased or hurt because of their Jewish dress.*

Q: How did they feel in the end?
A: *They felt proud to be Jewish and were happy they didn't hide their Jewishness.*

Q: Why did Yaakov compare their situation to the Holocaust?
A: *Yaakov compared their situation to the Jews in the Holocaust because some of the Jews then were trying to hide the fact that they were Jews and it didn't help them. They still were caught and killed by the Nazis Y"MSH.*

Q: What would you have done if it was you in the situation?

Q: Why do you think Hashem puts us in such situations?

Q: How could the story have turned out differently?
A: *They could have gotten hurt anyway, even though they were so brave. Sometimes Jews have to suffer for Kiddush Hashem.*

Thought Question

Q: When faced with danger or discomfort, do you think that you should hide the fact that you are Jewish?

10 The Miracle

Author's Reflections

Perhaps we should first determine what is a miracle. It would seem to me that any event or occurrence for which there is no reasonable or logical explanation may be deemed a miracle. Some miracles can be minor, some major, depending on the circumstances.

A student who gets an excellent grade on a test he was certain he was going to fail may think the results a miracle. Let's say, a minor miracle at least.

An avalanche of snow obliterates an entire mountain village, but leaves one small house untouched. No apparent physical cause for the avalanche to have been deflected leaving this one house to survive. A major miracle? Perhaps.

The story of Chanukah is told over and over again, and is especially poignant at the lighting of the menorah. How could a candle containing enough oil for perhaps one day burn for eight days? How could that happen?

The credibility of miracles is again asserted in the true story reported during the Sinai War of 1967.

It was a dark, moonless night when a small contingent of Israeli soldiers were confronted by a full regiment of Egyptians. The Israelis were cornered, their backs against vertical mountain walls. Facing them were the overpower enemy forces intent on their total destruction. There was no way out.

Instead of conceding defeat, the Israeli sergeant in charge demanded that the Egyptians surrender. After a moment's hesitation, the Egyptian commander, Colonel Hakim, gave up. To this day he swears that at least fifty Israeli tanks were standing ready to pummel his regiment. Tanks that did not exist.

I believe that every one of us can recall a time when an odd occurrence evoked the response, "That was nothing short of a miracle."

David had slain Goliath and Samson destroyed a small army of Philistines with the jawbone of a donkey.

Miracles do happen.

THIS *TRUE STORY* HAPPENED DURING THE *1967* SIX DAY WAR, AS TOLD BY MR. AZARIA BEN YITZCHAK NOW LIVING IN TULSA, OKLAHOMA.

In our prayers we say that G-d is the Master of all wars. Victory is not determined by the number of tanks, airplanes, soldiers or weapons. If G-d desires it, victory can be won by a small number of poorly armed soldiers against far greater numbers. He can do miracles and save the few from many, as He did during the time of Chanukah.

The real battle is to do what's right and find favor in Hashem's eyes. If we keep His mitzvos and act like a holy nation, Hashem promises to take care of us from all our external enemies.

Questions to Think About

Q: What was Isaac wondering about as he lit the Chanukah Menorah?
A: He was wondering how the miracle of the oil really happened.

Q: What is the miracle? Do you think that miracles can happen today?
A: A miracle is an occurrence for which there is no reasonable or logical explanation. Yes miracles can and do happen in this day and age. Our very existence is a miracle. From the smallest flower to the mightiest mountain all of creation is one miracle after another.

Q: What was the miracle in the story that happened in modern times?
A: An event that happened during the 1967 Sinai War.

Thought Question

Q: Why do you think Hashem makes outright miracles happen sometimes?

Q: Did any miracles or incredible occurrences ever happen in your life?

Q: Why do you think it happened?

11 The Right Decision

Author's Reflections

Call it providence or fate, but either can play an important role in our lives, often affecting others with whom we come in contact. This story should cause us to pause and consider acts that may result in benefits rather than negatives.

A positive outlook in a tough situation can help. More, it can be uplifting for life in general. What is the alternative? To constantly look at life's events through dark, smokey glasses that cast an unrelenting gloom over everything? A positive decision, a right decision can not only brighten our lives but the lives of those around us.

The story "The Right Decision" demonstrates that despite a less than happy beginning, Yaakov and Isaac turn a problem day into one that is rewarding. Not only for them, but also for strangers whose path they cross.

By not turning a deaf ear to a cry for help, they rescue a child in trouble. They could have ignored the plaintive call. They were already late for school. Why should they stop to investigate? It was probably nothing, and would only make them later to get to school. All logical reasons to let the call go unheeded.

But they made the right decision. They helped someone in trouble. And they eliminated the pain and suffering of frightened parents.

It is important to understand that any honest decision we make will be the right one. Each one of us has the innate sense to do the right thing. To make the right decision. We must never ignore a plea for help. Even if it is a hoax, better not to judge beforehand. Better to be fooled than to be sorry for not having helped. Yaakov and Isaac could never forgive themselves if they hadn't made the right decision.

47

Everyone is busy. Sometimes in the rush of taking care of our needs and wants, we come across others who need a helping hand. It's not always easy to respond, especially when we'll have to give up or miss something important to us.

But we cannot live only for ourselves. A call for help should never be ignored even if we have to put our interests momentarily on the back burner.

Questions to Think About

Q: What happened to Yaakov and Isaac on their way to school?
A: *They heard a very strange sound like someone crying.*

Q: What was the decision they had to make?
A: *They were already late for school and they could have gotten in big trouble for stopping to check out this crying sound. But they decided to check it out anyway.*

Q: Do you think that they did the right thing?
A: *Yes! You should always try and help people if you think they may be in trouble, even if you might be late for school or you have to do something else. Their actions in the story may very well have saved the young child's life - a very big mitzvah.*

Q: Why is it so important to help other people and put your own plans aside sometimes?
A: *We are all of us, Hashem's creations and we all have Hashem inside of us. The essence of Hashem as taught in the Torah is Chasdei Hashem - Hashem's kindness. Everything that Hashem created in the world was done out of his abiding kindness. Since we are all to emulate Hashem's ways and since we are all important, helping other people is also important. If we needed help ourselves, we would want other people to stop what they were doing and help us. Equally so, we must be prepared to do the same for others.*

Thought Question

Q: Did something like this ever happen to you?

Q: What did you do? Did you make the right decision?

12 The Bullies

Author's Reflections

Bullies come in all forms, shapes and sizes. They can be boys or girls, men or women. Most of us have experienced meeting a bully at one time or another. Perhaps in school or at the place where we work. Usually, a bully is one who himself feels inferior and attempts to prove his worth by intimidating someone smaller or weaker. Giving a reason for why someone is a bully does not alleviate the situation. The reason may be more complex if he is a Jew, and no less perplexing.

One should not allow himself to be bullied, but this story demonstrates that force should be used only as a last resort. Discussion should be backed with strength and determination. The domination by a bully is an unacceptable situation.

Sometimes, a bully may resort to verbal abuse rather than physical. But, verbal abuse can be equally as damaging and hurtful. A bully will say, "Oh, I was just having some fun. I meant no harm." Having fun at someone else's expense can cause harm. All of us should be conscious of the fact that any one of us can slip into the role of bully without fully realizing it.

Discussions and an attempt at understanding should be the first approach to stopping a bully's conduct. However, this has to backed up by more than words. If a bully's intent is to cause harm, then it must be made clear that harm will not go unpunished.

One only has to read a newspaper to know that bullies are a part of our daily lives. It is only a short step between bully and terrorist. By standing together when a bully threatens, the possibility of harm is diminished. But the bully cannot be allowed to vent his own inadequacies on the backs of others.

Do you know any bullies? Perhaps you should show him this story.

51

How does one stop a bully? You can try fighting him back, but does it make sense to take part in a cycle of unending violence? Sometimes having the support of friends and honest talk can defuse a bully and get him to rethink his behavior.

That's a lot better than every day putting on your boxing gloves, getting ready for a fight and hoping you don't get beaten up -- knowing you'll have to face a new round the next day.

Furthermore, the Torah teaches us the correct way to act in order to proctect ourselves, our firends, and our families when confronted with bullies or other such difficult situations.

In the story of the patriarch Yaakov, when he left his father-in-law's house and his entourage met his brother Esau, Yaakov took several actions that serve as a model for how we should try to act.

1) He davened (prayed) to Hashem to help him.

2) He divided his family into two separate groups, so Esau could not harm all of them at once

3) He prepared for a war with Esau

4) He sent gifts to appease and "befriend" Esau.

So, while we must always be prepared to defend ourselves, our family and friends and our values and beliefs, we should try to find other solutions just as Yaakov the patriarch did.

Questions to Think About

Q: Why do you think Tzvi lied to his Rebbe?
A: *Maybe he was embarrassed to tell the rebbe in front of everyone that he was beaten up by some bullies.*

Q: Do you think Tzvi did the right thing by going to Yaakov and Isaac for help?
A: *Yes, going for help is always good in these situations, but he probably should have told an adult as well.*

Q: Was Yaakov's idea of helping Tzvi a good one?
A: *Yes, the bullies realized that they were wrong and even agreed to be a part of the right team. They didn't use violence which showed the bullies that violence is wrong.*

Q: Why do you think bullies act the way they do?

A: *They may have problems of their own or they feel inferior and need to prove themselves. There are always other and better ways to prove yourself, such as positive outlets like hobbies or sport, and of course, learning. Being the best you can be and trying as hard as you can in every situation. Everyone has their own special gifts and strengths. Learning what yours are and growing stronger in your special area makes you a better person and better able to serve Hashem in your own special way.*

Thought Question

Q: Did you ever face a bully? What happened to you? How did you deal with the bully?

13 You Have a Choice

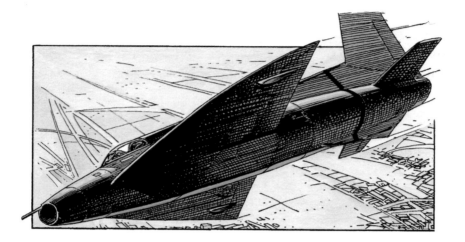

Author's Reflections

Part of the pleasure in doing these "Yaakov and Isaac" stories is my belief that they can be entertaining, beneficial and thought-provoking for the readers. As a father and a grandfather I've tried to communicate these basic ideas to my children, hoping it will enable them to make wise choices and decisions in their lives.

Here, again, Rabbi Pape supplied me with the details and pertinent information on how to make a home kosher. When I was a child growing up, a kosher home was a natural setting for me, but making a home kosher was a new experience. Cooking vessels must be heated to red-hot, while plates and eating utensils must be boiled. Porcelain and china must be refired in kilns *if at all*. What a job! But no one ever said it was easy to be Jewish.

For me, this story has much wider ramifications.

Often, life decisions are made with too little information and may lead to unhappy results. Being an airplane pilot or a deep sea diver may sound exciting and romantic. Even heroic. But, what does a person have to do in order to earn those titles? Do we realize the years of study, work and dedication involved in order to pursue various careers?

I'm reminded of a young man I recently met who expressed a desire to become a cartoonist. He was inspired by an animated cartoon which ignited an unfulfilled ambition. The thought of doing an animated cartoon and having a world audience see it was so exciting that he was ready to do it. Or, so he thought.

To become a cartoon animator one must be able to draw everything and anything. The simple drawings seen on a movie screen may look easy to do, but quite the opposite is true. In addition to drawing ability, the animator must be knowledgeable in the use of computers and many other kinds of technical equipment involved in producing modern cinematic animation. Before making a commitment it is essential that the individual make an informed choice. Learn as much as you can about the subject before you make a decision, and the decision will be based on the acquisition of considerable information.

This story of making a home kosher is one of these very important decisions.

YOU HAVE A CHOICE

© 1987 JOE KUBERT

NOTE: BEFORE KOSHERING ANYTHING, A COMPETANT RABBINIC AUTHORITY SHOULD BE CONSULTED.

The End

55

The essence of being a Jew is keeping Torah and Mitzvahs, which of course includes the mitzvah of keeping kosher. Yet, Hashem still gives us the ability to freely choose our path in life. There are many people who have never experienced a truly Jewish and Kosher home. For such people, koshering their home is indeed part of learning and making an informed choice. In order to do so, learning and studying Judaism provides the basis for making such a choice. Similarly, every step of our path in life should be approached with caution, learning and evaluating. Getting information before making an important decision in life is indeed like kashering one's kitchen. The parallel would be to tell a Jew to study Judaism before he decides whether to keep kosher or not.

Kashering his kitchen doesn't give information on which to decide whether to keep mitzvos or not, but is the result of receiving information and deciding that it is important.

The Talmud tells us that there are 600,000 "faces to the Torah", meaning that within the realm of Halacha, there can be equally correct yet differing opinions. These can vary for example, as between Ashkenazic (European) versus Sephardic (Middle-Eastern) traditions and customs. In the story, a certain opinion was expressed even though there may be differing viewpoints. It is important to note, in all cases, a competent Rabbi should be consulted before making Koshering or other decisions.

Questions to Think About

Q: What jobs were Yaakov and Isaac talking about with the Rabbi in the story.
A: *An Astronaut and an engineer.*

Q: What was the Rabbi trying to teach the boys about making choices of what you want to become in life?
A: *When you are making a choice of what to do in life, you have to first know many things about the job. After you know everything you have to know, then you can decide if that job is right for you. If you don't learn about the job first, then you might make the wrong decision and you could end up being very unhappy. Of course, whatever path you take, you should always set aside a fixed time for learning Torah each day. Also, make sure you talk it over with a competent Rabbi.*

Q: Why do you think Mr. Zangara decided to become Kosher? Becoming Kosher is very difficult to do.
A: *Mr. Zangara wants to follow Hashem and the mitzvahs of the Torah. This is why he would do difficult tasks in order to become Kosher.*

Q: Why do you think the Rabbi in the story told the boys they should learn Torah first and then decide what the want to do with their lives?
A: *Learning Torah teaches Jews what Hashem wants them to do. Once you know what Hashem wants, it is easy to make the right decisions. We all should try and do what Hashem wants us to do because He's the one who created us and Who runs the world.*

14 The Rope of Life

Author's Reflections

The basis for this story was told to me by Rabbi Pape. It concerns old age, but I believe it applies to all of us regardless of age.

The story's origin goes back thousands of years, to the time of the Roman Emperor Hadrian. Passing through the city of Tiberias, he came upon a very old man working in the fields. He was impressed by the fact that the old man was laboring under a hot sun, despite his advanced years.

"Why do you work so hard, grandfather?" scoffed the Emperor. "Is it not time for you to rest, to eat the fruits of your labor?"

The old man answered, "As long as I am alive, I must do what I can."

"How old are you?" asked the Emperor.

"Almost 100 years old," the old man answered.

"But you are planting trees whose fruit you will never eat."

"Then my children will eat. How much longer I live and of my usefulness, only Hashem knows."

The point is that none of us knows how long we will live, but that we should be as productive as long as possible. Who knows the benefits that may be derived from our efforts or how they will apply to us or those close to us?

In the story I've illustrated, the old fisherman braids his rope despite the prevailing bad weather. He should be inside a warm place, huddled near a fire, having a good meal. Instead, he works as he has in years past. Perhaps by continuing to work he feels more a part of the world around him. Perhaps he is so accustomed to working it would be more difficult for him to stop than to go on.

So, when a young boy falls into the water, the old fisherman is there to save him. If the old man had been at home, perhaps the boy might have drowned. None of us knows when or how we may be called upon to exercise our usefulness. We should never discount a person's abilities because of age or physical shortcomings. The young should learn the valuable lessons garnered from the experience of our elders, as others who follow will learn from us.

As the old fisherman says, "We are all sailors braiding the rope of life…"

The End

A person should strive to be productive throughout his life. It is not only a question of making money to support oneself, but making the world a better place for everyone.

Just as all of us are benefiting from a world made more comfortable by the inventors and doers who came before us, we should seek to make the world a better place for those who will come after us.

There is a famous story from several years ago, about a venerable Rabbi who was flying to Israel from NY. he traveled in business class and happened to be sitting next to the former Foreign Minister of Israel. The Foreign Minister couldn't help but notice how the Rabbi's son, a middle aged man himself, who was sitting in economy class, continually hovered near his father. He wouldn't let the stewardess take care of his father's simple travel comforts, including bringing him water, arranging his pillow, or other efforts on his fatehr's behalf.

The Foreign Minister said to the Rabbi, he was impressed that the son was so attentive to the Rabbi. He mentioned his own son, about the same age as the Rabbi's son, rarely had anything to do with him, to his sorrow. The Rabbi replied that it is an outcome of their differing world-views. The Foreign Minister comes from a more "modern" world where everything is youth oriented. Newer is better. In the modern secular world, each succeeding generation is held to be better than the preceeding generation. Therefore, the Foreign Minister's son, sees no reason to show respect for the older generation.

However, The Jewish world-view is, since the generation of Sinai was the pinacle of our civilization, each succeeding generation is one more step removed from that greatness. Therefore, the Rabbi's son realizes that he is less than his father, who is one generation closer to the perfection of Sinai.

As Yaakov and Isaac learned, you have to show great respect to the older generation, where there is deep experience and wisdom. Indeed, the Torah tells us we must show respect for our elders.

Questions to Think About

Q: Why do you think the old man was outside working on such a cold, nasty night?
A: *Maybe because it makes him feel useful working, even though he is so old.*

Q: Do you think that older people should continue working?
A: *Older people contribute a lot to society. If they are able to continue working then it makes them feel better about themselves and we learn a lot from their wisdom. Our sages "work" in Torah all their lives, setting us the example of how we should live our lives.*

Q: When the old fisherman saves the young boys life in the story, what do we learn from this?
A: *It doesn't matter how old a person is or what he looks like. Everyone of us has a very important role to play in life. Our sages tell us that Hashem will never ask us why we were not like Moses or Abraham or King David. He will ask us why we weren't ourselves. Why we didn't reach for and attain our own potential, our role in the rope of life.*

Thought Question

Q: Was there a time when an older person has helped you? Did you appreciate this help at the time? We must all have Hakores Hatov (gratitude) for people who have helped us. Have you given the proper respect to your parents, grandparents and elders?

15 An Act of Kindness

"SOME OF THE HORSES SUCCEEDED--THEN-- *TURNED BACK* INTO THE RAGING WATER TO HELP THEIR WEAKER BROTHERS!"

Author's Reflections

The subjects that were suggested for this story are the outstanding principles of love and kindness described in the five books of the Bible, the Torah. It is an especially important idea to communicate to children, since cruelty can be displayed inadvertently or unintentionally by the young. A puppy or a kitten may be mishandled by a child. They need to learn all living creatures, even insects, should not be abused.

With this thought in mind, I felt that an animal of noble stature would be a proper catalyst for this message of kindness. And that I should make the comparison between the powerful horse and the smallest, most timid creature, a bird.

It was important to point out that even the lowest of animals feel pain -- and love. The example given in the story of the horses helping one another is true. The strong should always help the weak because that exemplifies the kind of courage for which we should all strive.

I tried to make the pictures both exciting and entertaining. I felt the readers would enjoy the story and its message would be painlessly absorbed. Hurting an animal is only a step away from hurting people. It's an important lesson for us all.

"THEY WERE HARD, CRUEL MEN, ISAAC... AND THEY PICKED THEIR HORSES *CAREFULLY*... FROM THE WILD HERDS THAT ROAMED THEIR COUNTRY! IT WAS NOT AN EASY TASK..."

"FIRST THEY CIRCLED THE HERD AND DROVE THEM INTO A DEEP, SWIFT RIVER ...KNOWING THAT ONLY THE *STRONG* ONES WOULD SURVIVE THE CURRENT!"

"SOME OF THE HORSES SUCCEEDED--THEN-- *TURNED BACK* INTO THE RAGING WATER TO HELP THEIR WEAKER BROTHERS!"

"THESE COURAGEOUS ANIMALS WERE THE WARRIORS' *FIRST CHOICE!* THESE HORSES WERE STRONG--AND *NOBLE!*"

EVEN *HORSES* CAN SHOW LOVE FOR ONE ANOTHER ... AND THIS IS A GREAT GENERAL PRINCIPAL OF OUR TORAH!

YOU SEE. ISAAC... BEING CRUEL TO *ANIMALS* IS ONLY A SHORT STEP AWAY FROM BEING CRUEL TO *PEOPLE!*

The End

The Bible tells us that G-d wants us to be compassionate, kind and righteous. These qualities should influence how we deal with our fellow man and even how we treat animals. Like humans, animals also feel pain and love, and suffer when they are mistreated. A person who treats an animal cruelly is maybe capable of treating a human the same way.

King Solomon teasches us in Proverbs, that we can learn many things from the animals. Animals are also capable of compassion. For instance, horses and dogs have been faithful to their masters even to the point of sacrificing themselves. If even animals show compassion to each other and to their human masters, shouldn't humans show compassion to them too?

Furthermore, one of the cardinal prinicpals of the Torah is "tzaar Baalei Chaim" not just not showing cruelty to animals. The Torah commands us that we are not even to EAT BREAKFAST ourselves until we have first seen to the needs of the animals under our care. Throughout the Torah are instances where travelers such as Eliezer and Jacob, saw first to the needs of their camels before they drank water themselves. How different is the cruel treatment of the warriors to the horses. These were skilled, yet hard and cruel warriors. Hashem teaches us that this treatement of his creatures is unacceptable. And, so we see as Yaakov says in the story, that ill treatment of animals can indeed lead to worse treatment of people.

Questions to Think About

Q: What is the important lesson in this story?
A: *The Torah teaches us it is a mitzvah not to be cruel to animals.*

Q: Why shouldn't we be cruel to animals?
A: *All of Hashem's creatures have feelings of pain and love.*

Q: Give an example of an animal feeling love in the story. Now try to think of your own example.
A: *The horse in the story felt love for the weaker horses. The Gemorah gives us an example of a poor farmer who sold his milk cow to a gentile. The cow would not give milk on the Shabbos. The Gentile called the farmer who whispered in the cows ear that he no longer belonged to the farmer and could now give milk on the Shabbos. Such is the loyalty and love that animals will have for Man if man treats them with love and respects that they too come from Hashem.*

Q: Why do you think the author used the mighty horse and the tiny bird for his examples?
A: *To show us that it doesn't matter how large or small a living being is, we still should not hurt it. Even insects should not be treated cruelly. Remember that King David himself was saved by a simple spider and showed Hakores Hatov to it.*

Thought Question

Q: Have you seen children being cruel to animals? What can you do to try to stop them and teach them that this is not right to do?

In the spring of 1926 Joe's mother, father and two year old sister Ida, left the small town of Wzeran in eastern Poland and after a brief stop in Southampton, England where Joe was born on Sept 18 1926, the Kubert's came to the new world – America, two months later.

Joe started to draw as soon as he was old enough to hold anything that would make a mark. When he was three or four, neighbor's would buy boxes of penny chalk for him to draw pictures in the street - in the gutters actually. The side walks were rough concrete but the gutters were smooth black macadam and better than slate blackboards for chalk. Joe always wanted to be a cartoonist from the time he saw his first comic strip in the newspapers before he could even read the words. The pictures pulled him into a world that he came to love. For Joe, the cartoon characters were alive, and weren't two dimensional brightly colored drawings outlined in black.
Joe wanted to do draw stories with figures that were alive.He learned to draw pictures like that - kind of magical.

Joe's father always encouraged him from the time he started to draw. This was unusual since most people "from the old country" would disuade their children from "wasting time scribbling" instead of aspiring themselves to something that would earn them a living like being a plumber or a carpenter or an electrician. Forget about doctor or lawyer that was for families that could afford college.
Joe's parents recognized his love for drawing and knew that it would be a lost cause to stop him. They gained a pride in Joe's ability and on the complements of family and strangers on his drawings

Joe got his first paying job as a cartoonist for comic books at the age of 11 1/2 or 12 years at five dollars a page working for Harry "A" Chesler's comic-book production house. In 1938 that was a lot of money. By 1940 Joe was making more money than His father who was a kosher butcher. He has never been unemployed - for even one day - since that time. He has worked in the field ever since, and in his more than sixty years with the medium he has produced countless stories for countless characters, including those in this book and DC Comics' Batman and many others. He also edited, wrote and illustrated the DC title *Sgt Rock* for thirty years.

During the last few years in particular, Joe has experienced the thrilling exhilaration of seeing his work published, knowing that hundreds of thousands of people were looking at it maybe with similar feelings such as the magic, Joe experienced when he saw comic strips for the first time so many years ago.

Mr. Kubert was a principal in the creation of the first 3-D comic book and his pioneering development of 3-D comic-book craft continued with the early appearances of what would become his best-known creation—a heroic caveman named Tor. Kubert was also one of the first authors to adapt the long-form version of comics that became known as graphic novels, these works include a graphic novel of Tor, the historical adventures of *Abraham Stone*, and the real-life story: *Fax From Sarajevo*. Kubert also contributed to the comic-strip industry. During the 1960s, he illustrated *Tales of the Green Beret* for the Chicago-Tribune New York News Syndicate.

In 1976, Kubert also founded the first and only accredited school devoted solely to the art of cartoon graphics. The Joe Kubert School of Cartoon and Graphic Art, Inc. in Dover, New Jersey, has since produced many of today's leading cartoonists. Pursuing this educational path further, in 1998 Kubert established a series of correspondence courses under the banner of Joe Kubert's World of Cartooning. At the same time, he established his website:

October 2003 saw publication of Mr. Kubert's two most recent long-form works: Including YOSSEL, written and illustrated by Mr. Kubert.

Currently, Kubert is producing PS Magazine for the U.S. Army and working on a graphic novel about gangsters in Brooklyn's East New York in the 1930s.

Kubert has received numerous awards, and over the years, has been the Guest of Honor to various Comic Conventions. Joe is a member of:

International Museum of Cartoon Art - Advisory Board
New York Press Club
Society of Illustrators
Advisory Board - Valley National Bank
National Cartoonist Society - Past Vice-President

Joe Kubert and his wife, Muriel, live in New Jersey. Two of their five children, Adam and Andy, have achieved great notoriety as comic-book artists.

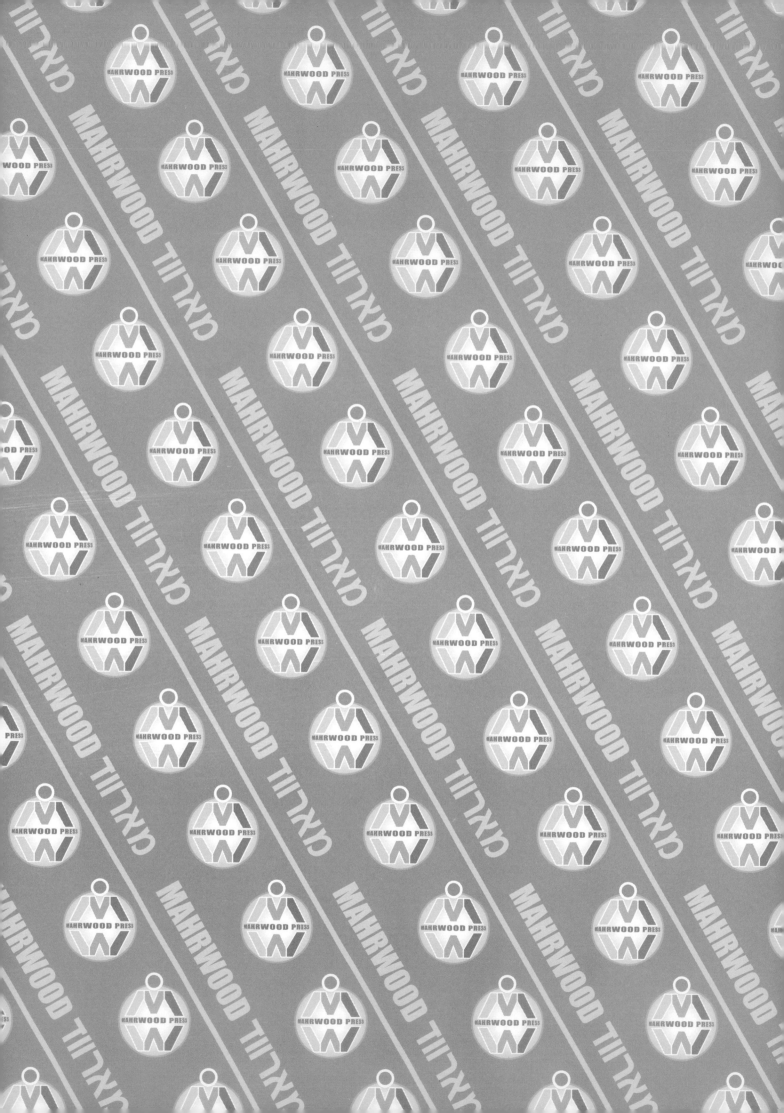